BAD MANNERS

For Rachel - L.G.

For Danny, Sarah and Joe - M.B.

First published in Great Britain in 2014 by
Piccadilly Press, a Templar/Bonnier publishing company
Deepdene Lodge, Deepdene Avenue, Dorking, Surrey RH5 4AT
www.piccadillypress.co.uk

Designed by Simon Davis
Printed and bound by WKT in China
Colour reproduction by Dot Gradations

ISBN: 978 1 84812 235 2 (hardback)
ISBN: 978 1 84812 234 5 (paperback)

1 3 5 7 9 10 8 6 4 2

A catalogue record of this book is available from the British Library

BAD MANNERS, BENJIE!

BY LYNNE GARNER
ILLUSTRATED BY MIKE BROWNLOW

Piccadilly

Boris had a new friend called Benjie.

Boris really liked Benjie . . .

but he didn't like his manners.

One morning, Benjie came for breakfast.
As they ate their food, Boris slurped and slobbered.
"Mmm, this is nice," he said, his mouth bulging
with green worm porridge.

Benjie waited until he'd swallowed his mouthful.
"Yes it is," he replied, wiping a small dribble
of porridge from his chin. "Thank you."

Just then, Boris felt his belly
mumble and grumble, grumble and rumble.
That was the trouble with eating
green worm porridge.
He gave a very loud,

BURP!

Boris looked at Benjie and waited.
Dog looked at Benjie and waited.
But Benjie kept eating his breakfast.

Boris said quietly, so only Dog could hear,

"He didn't even try to do a better burp!"

Later, they decided to go for a swim.

As they got to the bus stop, Boris felt his belly burble and bubble, bubble and gurgle. Boris did the smelliest pumpf you've ever smelt.

Boris looked at Benjie and waited.

Dog looked at Benjie and waited.

But Benjie said nothing.

Boris said quietly, so only Dog could hear,

"He didn't even say what a good trouser trump that was!"

After a little while, the bus juddered to a stop and an
old troll heaved himself on. The old troll grumbled
because all the seats were full.

"Have my seat," offered Benjie, standing up.

Boris and Dog looked on in astonishment.

Who gave up their seat like that?

When the bus got to the lake, Boris, Dog and Benjie got off. Everyone was pushing, shoving and elbowing each other out of the way.

When Boris got into the water, he saw Benjie
still standing on the bank, waiting patiently.
"I'm going to have to say something
to Benjie," said Boris to himself.

A little later, when they were enjoying a red bug ice cream in the park, Benjie felt his nose tingle and tickle, tickle and prickle. He pulled out a huge, crisp, clean white handkerchief.

ATISHOO!

Boris looked at Benjie and waited.
Dog looked at Benjie and waited.

But Benjie folded up his handkerchief
and put it back into his bag.
Boris said quietly, so only Dog could hear,
"He didn't even look at his bogey!"

Boris heard a small troll say, "Did you see that?"
"Yes," replied her friend, looking shocked. "What a waste!"
"I know," said the small troll. "Just think of all the things
you can do with a good bogey!"

"I used my last one as a bouncy ball,"
said the small troll's brother, throwing it up
in the air for everyone to see.

"Benjie," said Boris, "it's embarrassing to be seen with you."

"Why?" asked Benjie.

"Look at you! You eat with your mouth closed, you don't burp, you don't trouser trump, you give up your seat, you wait your turn, you waste good bogeys . . ." said Boris.

"You have the manners of a

of a . . .

"...a HUMAN!" said Boris, in despair.

"No I don't!" said Benjie, looking hurt.

"Yes you do," said Boris. "Even Dog thinks so."

"Really?" Benjie asked Dog.

Dog nodded.

Just then, Benjie's nose began to tingle and tickle, tickle and prickle again.

He sneezed an enormous sneeze into his handkerchief.

ATISHOOOOOOO!

Dog looked at Benjie and waited.

Boris looked at Benjie and waited.

Benjie stared at the big blue bogey.

Then he peeled off the bogey and
popped it into his mouth.
"Mmm," he said chewing.

"That's MUCH better," said Boris smiling.

"At last you have the manners of a troll!"